Revelation: love and death

David Lott

Revelation: love and death

Ideate Media
(https://ideatemedia.wordpress.com)

Introduction

Varied and lucid, the poems in this series depict a history, a journey. They begin with a portrayal of innocence, marked by a desire to please others and by a limited ability to understand and evaluate experience. Then, in part 2, they present moments of essentials and permanents, to serve as a foundation for judgement and assessment in the final part. In the final part, the poems explore the worlds of imagination and reality in the ongoing effort to develop the spirit of the self, whilst also charting the loss of innocence and of uncertainty. In the course of this journey, there's a twist or two that you might not expect.

Contents

Part 3
In and out of time

Part 1

Bits of time

paralysis

It was as when they said he's ill
and I walked to him wondering,
racing in a limbo – what
to expect, how react.

But, when I saw his new silent paralysis,
stoked and struck,
I held the frightened hand that'd moulded me
and waited, in his forced silence,
who had listened despite,
and, afterwards, grief came a prickly pelt.
It was as when the phallus,
aware of its mere velleity,
bends and drifts, and then
sucked, would pound as a caged seal
into a new pool,
and sees the deep violet there – it knows,
receding, as the mind laughs blind.

It was as, at Majdanek, I walk
thoughtless down the middle aisle
to the mound of ash and the ground beyond
scabrous with guilty lumps,
and the stacked beds like racks where the stench
no wind will dissipate,
of plank and tray and wire and stove and tap and
scratched slab;
as the haze fades behind the watch towers,
I walk past the shoes and showers and, nerved to

it, to where
Death concentrated in a room – the *penseur*.
The rough grass tended, the oven house locked,
I leave it like the dead mad,
glowing upwards and backwards,
nod to platitudes,
intellect at ironies,
accept no sensibility that can refine and rest it.
It was as when the thought caught in the synapse
sought for a shape and a link and, then,
the character was richer than the conception,
the symbol tenser than the image.

It was as when, at the Sagrada, when
the builder's sleep raw with voices shaped
bold sculptures to melt away like lava,
and children dropped from fairground towers.
Mazes
rise into space and steps step
down into air, where, realised, the tourist
later peers
into the builder's dreams.

It was as when your love marries away,
and the bridegroom is complimented and
his laugh rings off the chessboard floors
and is absorbed in the thought of statues
half-lodged in walls. The desire has no
object now and the turning on itself
is a kid of limp malice and peace, and all
dreaming is in

black and white.

It was as when they said he's ill
and I walked to him wondering;
it was as when
I would hold the will
to hold the frightened hand.

kind of

It's like –
d'you know the feeling? –
standing at a cliff edge
and your body leans forward.

To fall would be
a letting-go of mask and of self.
I know I won't go mouthing
unheard, a brief and sharp singing
in my head.

I may drop
in incomplete phrases
and lie there, laid open.
I may think back,
curved back on the rock,
my arm crooked at the elbow, fingers kneeling.

Or, I might glide and then
float, for the air was open
and I took it
and it forms an oil,
a thrust of warmth,
a care, kind of

exhilaration

When you have moved so close that
you can smell it and sense
the sweat in it,
and see how you like it and
see how it likes you,
like stepping into the cold and lap of the sea,
only then can it be known.
When you have leant against it
full frontal,
it rocks back like a host and says
'Hi, here I am. Feel me. Let me up you.'
And it thrusts forward and says 'Shall we play?'
And it says 'Okay, let's try some weight.
Here's a ledge. That was easy.
Let's rock some more. And here's a hand-hold
right up here. And here's a smooth saucer for
your toe.' And the crack between the
blades, as the arms jack the muscles
to stand out in the sun. And a new
point to a new ledge where the foot is cupped.
And puzzling the next lift,
it sits with the creases of its stomach bare to the
air, and feels the grip of your toe in
its elephant hide,
and watches in contention
and tires at the waiting.
And breathes out
as each time, each puzzle is broken,
from ledge to ledge

all the way to the top,
where the wind and the sun play
in vertigo.

hiss

Silver and blued copper, quicksilver stream
of the leaves seething in the rush and
frantic of the scattered wind,
the flicking of the long grass,
the swell and tide of fields,
splaying of the rain in mud wood ,
air playing with the tension of the trees in line
along the summered ridge
where branch grates on new-touched bark
within the simmer and leaf-fold hiss

Pure and unchanging, the constant sound
of managed air where pressure dulls the
lower sounds, a service air
that serves a service smile, the constant
hiss above the clouds whose great
columns will be circled round
in rapt attention to each change of sound,
each lowering hum
that beckons the ground

The slim whisper that comes up from the sand
and turns to a rant in the spray and cresting,
the water that pulls the sand away
to each new building of the rolling
and hits the inner drum so hard
it hisses there and hisses there
in the silent of a thought-stopped night

nameless

A red-tailed catfish,
with eyes on the top of its head
and three flexing whiskers,
leant against its windows of glass

Its tank was more of a room
in a pale shade of blue –
no stones, no weeds, no pretence –
the home of an ascetic

It lay on the glass,
tail bent to one side,
soft in its fish fat,
its black and white skin almost furry

It stared without blinking
at those who came to its neck of the shop,
the part of the world its presence had filled

In the bulbous white of one eye
was a deep red vein

It once had been sold, it said on a note
on the glass,
but had wasted away
and, to try and revive him,
they'd returned it to here,
to the muffled sounds,
to review and consider the visitors

Human and fish silently study the other
and seek for some point of understanding

Or, maybe he reads me
better than I him;
he need not negotiate;
he's wider and shrewder than me –
me, just another fish, stranded and with bloodshot
in my eye

gifts

You bring me presents.
You ask me what I want.
I browse the shops for you.

I like your gifts
but like you more;
I feel they are a half-way ground – somewhere
between love and liking,
and wait for when you may say to me:
How do you want me?

purport

He expresses himself smoothly –
his meaning is plain,
   but she sees
   the thought in his mind.

He stays in his head
and speaks with his eyes
   and she waits, till she cracks
   through the pressure of days.

He strains for the words
that will not be found
   and she hears his heart
   that is ticking behind
      and trusts to a feeling
      that seems sure.

And when he is past
and the world is all gone,
   he will see what he spent
   in lonely debating,
      that should have been lived in
      taking and giving.

hymn

She spreads her fingers,
she raises one arm above her head
and holds her hair;
the cloth wraps round
below her navel, her belly,
in the thunderplay of afternoon

She cups her breast
and lowers her head –
she plays in my head
as morning siren, as model to Matisse.
I long for her
to turn her lips towards me
and like the salt-sea spray
to kiss me.

I pray that she will come
and that I will be firm;
I pray that my love for her
is strong, is pure.

planting

Startled the little tree,
as it looked up at me,
feeling the print
of my hand and my breath,
its young stem and slight branches
thorny and callow

When I held it in place in the
hole I had dug,
the earth slipped away from its roots.
Pale and secret, they fractured the air,
like a litter of kittens
disturbed in their hiding.
I hid them again and buried them down
to passage and grow
and hold tight to the wind, and
watered the mud to a sheen –
startled the tree
when it looked up at me.

the spaces

I saw   love
as taking.
I said   this is my love
and you must share   your fruits
with me.
You must not   question.
You must not   disagree.
Love is not
liking.

This   is the kind of love I know,
the love   I   have received
the love that   glowers in the night
that I give   to you.

I said you   are my love,
I give   as   you give.
Love is giving and   taking.
And I saw the silken whorl draw up   and in
and lock tight, a mossy
grey around the
bright stem, and heart withdrawn
to a world   where I could not go.
I knew you to your nemesis,   all words,
all abstract   and
abstracted.

And who shall give?
And who shall   take?

And who is giving, and who is   equal
In their taking?

Blocked, I   relented
and then I sensed   love,
fasting   at the feast
silence   in a symphony
a wealth of   nothing
an effort   of ease.

Love stands   naked,
arms full
of gifts.

at the returns counter

As we ask to return
What we thought we wanted,
With our minds on our thoughts
Like our shoes on our feet,
Can we think of the nude
That lives under our clothes?
Can we think of the song
That our soul wants to sing,
And the history it tells
Of our past and our future,
Even think of the night
When our skin will be touched
By a beam from the sun
That has bounced off a rock
On the moon?

funeral words

At times like this, we may look through books
for the perfect words,
to give form to our feelings and
make the thing complete,
set the matter at rest.
Yet in hours of searching
each piece lies rejected –
too precise, too difficult, too sweet,
too harsh, implying what we do not wish
to say. But look into the grey wide sky
and the thoughts will come
like this:

Remember me when I loved you most
and you loved me most,
remember me when I was my bravest
when I did you right,
then let that be our secret bond
and, just once, let us rise in the morning
and enjoy the light
and know that that bird in the mist
is returning to the sun.

an occasional poem

In the bleak midwinter
I remember when we walked in that day that
lengthened straight from dawn to dusk, and
we collected wood along the path, loading
the pushchair

frosty wind made moan
Well, no, it didn't, it was still, but cold
in a straight-in-your face way, like
the beginnings of a pub fight, and
some people walked past us and one said:
"so, gathering winter fewel",
with that Wenceslas style of
few-el

earth stood hard as iron
Well, not really that either, that day, but
I can remember other days,
pre-Christmas days, post-Christmas days, where
the mother of mud is
tough but brittle like ...
like iron rust around etched and frosted
panes of water

water like a stone
The freezer is accreting Christmas lists,
its whiteness etched
with thoughts of things to come,
little frozen moments of delight

that may stay that way or,
one day, silent and hidden, melt

snow had fallen, snow on snow
Yes, once it did from after the magic of Guy
Fawkes to the earnest nativity,
and then the buttered light
light in the church where, with the passage of
youth, a quavering voice cracked on the top note
of 'Once in royal',
yes, right there, in the heaven-composed,
face-solemnity of the knowing-eyed soloist,
who yet could still accept the virgin birth
with ease

snow on snow
hey, what did he know or could accept otherwise,
and Jesus
seemed just a brother or a dad or
some doppelganger, but Israel ...

in that blank world, Israel wasn't
a people or a place – it was the story of a soul,
my soul, your soul,
the story of its trial.
But that was ...

in the bleak midwinter
long ago

the idle time

Before the feeling contract
is found exploded – a shrinkle rag of plastic
from a shining blue balloon,

Before the crag-haired double-dealing, two
minds locked in lovestrokewar,

Before the nights of silence,
effigies laid apart on stone beds

Before the morning dew of smiling
and quiet words,

Before the fond procession
of seeding and breeding,
the nights of waking, the
fugal breathing,
the drowsily proffered breast,
and the wince at the limpet grab
of young gums,

Before the urgent attention to the
call of private places,

Before the secret exchange of keys
that will turn the locks on needs,

Before the invitation, before
the link of eye-thoughts across a room,

Then there is the idle time, the shiny
engine rippling the coachwork
and, deep inside, the sieve that waits
for the flour
to trickle through.

spiritual

You say, when I use the word,
that she, my she, uses it too –
you say "what does it mean?"

And this, when leaning against the backdoor post,
you roll a roll-up and other thoughts
wander round my head,
playing with the distance in our age,
feeling your youth, your relative youth,
wanting to sustain your journey,
thinking of our near-strangers' intimacy,
and I telling you of too many things that are dear
and never opened,
like a child with a tale or two to tell,
but then I strain for inspiration,
the freezing air scratching at my nape and wrists

We return to the warmth and our others
and to calm the unease I say
"we discussed the spiritual,
and what is that".
Your he says it's the movement away from hard
memories, a separation.
My she says it's the link when mind and body
become one.
Splitting off and melding –
it is, it seems, two opposites in one

But, as you rise from the sofa and leave the room,

I think it may be the little wishes,
the hesitancies, that danced around us,
like ghosts of summer butterflies,
in the winter air.

tempted

"Posso" they say and they mean
I could, not I may

They do not toy with
chance, do not relish
velleity, English soufflé

As you bend forward, place
your hands on the table
and let 'carpe diem' fall,
a crystal of choices splash between us,
I look to your eyes
but through the fallen neck of cloth, at the
blurred edge watch the curve and double
of beauty held forth and nestled and
linked

Posso

This sets conscience at play for words of
commitment made in a yellowed moment. This
pricks and rests my desire,
Seeing a bank by the river
And sitting on rugs on grass that rises like
hair on the skin
near the flow of the water

Posso

In a walled and silent back alley, to
myself, posso I say
but I mean
I may, not I could

Non posso

her and him

It had seemed, at first,
through the passage of the early days,
like a circling round –
her gravitation to him,
his to her

A curving round through time,
each never quite knowing,
never quite touching
soul to soul –
each hoping –
in a kind of helix, undoubled.

Did he start to wonder?
Did she?
Who first?
But, so, they felt no prompt,
they felt no pull,
and the lines became parallel,
no risk of touching –
two planes of self, ranging on
through a plague of time.

And the lines began to kink,
the line of him and the line of her,
to snake, to veer,
and the trundling carriage
buckled at the axis
of what they thought they had.

Each is a single wheel now,
on single lines that bend and lean
ever more apart, that can carry
nothing more than each alone –
sometimes seeming going nowhere –
each wondering
who they were
and where they went.

Florentine debate

He looked, to me, both serene and troubled – the
David, the Davide.
Maybe the feeling of being adored and admired
was, in the rock-captured moment,
turning to some perplexity, touchy even – maybe
because he was, in the end,
not the wonder, and not the worker of the marvel,
but just Davide,
and of the marble, and no more;
after standing hour after hour,
through the scratching and
the blank echoing of the hammering,
maybe he felt as chiselled,
as overawed, as used, maybe.
In time, perhaps, he felt too much the giver,
and not the given.

I looked down at my own little one. She
looked anguished too;
she spoke fitfully, her mind still
on yesterday's waves near Pisa,
on the tingle they gave.
She felt a long way from the sea, I guessed,
a long way from her bucket
and her spade.

We looked at the back of it –
of him – and saw the tooling still in the stone.
We saw the chisel drive

and the hammer shock still there.

"This is rock like skin or skin like rock."
"And what can you do with that?" she said,
bumpily.
"Take one thing and make it like another –
the craft of the impossible," I said.
"Why?"

We walked on – our minds on the seaside splash
and cackle,
on the way the water talked to you,
worked its quiet way around you,
like cream encircling a strawberry,
like the passage of time
on the fruit of a vine.

searching

I walked from the warmth, the couch,
along a street of rented rooms
of shades of oatmeal
of hard reds,
from where feelings are made gods
where charity and commerce meet,
gentleness and subjection,
through the dark gloom of a lamp,
sharp sprays of light in the puddles
before the glow of shut rooms
ripe with coffee, with bargaining, with love.

My mind is tired. Tired of itself.
And my body walks. Walks hard.
The body that feeds the mind with shadows,
that free-falls when it spins the world.

I can think no more of individuals, of scenes,
of feelings that I owned.
They are laid to rest for now.
I see abstractions, purities, hidden truths.
I work to wake myself one mind,
not thought and feeling,
wish and action.

In this little world of petals, of hedges,
of lawns clipped,
it seems as if clear
that what is hard father to the self

must let the self re-father it.

The greatest bliss would be in the morning
waking,
carried gently to the shore by the dreaming sea,
to lie there in the surf and listen
and live with the world
as a charmed place.

Part 2

Outside time

abstract with feeling

Courage is a square shape.
Love is triangular.
And, when two triangles
meet and form square,
then courage is born –
the true shape of love.
Hatred is heart-shaped,
for hearts can never
form in seamless tiling.
Circles are the love of self.

question

If I am the light
then there is no darkness
If I am the truth
then there is no doubt
If I am the answer
there is no more a question
there is no more a life
for life is only life through doubt and night

I am a question
A new question
And a new question holds within itself
a quest,
a new journey

death in the office

I'd been thinking about the passage of time,
and how (watching the clock
prowl around the hours) an hour
could be a year, while a year
could seem an hour,
and, so,
I was glad to see him.

Death hadn't knocked;
he'd just slipped the door open, sleekly.

He set down opposite me,
arranging his robes about him, and
lit a cigarette, like he owned the place,
which, in a way, he did.

"I've been thinking about you," he said;
"you know I come to everyone,
but I don't like to come to those
who have not lived."

His skin had a yellow tinge,
a moistened papyrus look.
"Why don't you get out of here?
Soon. Why don't you go somewhere?" he asked
looking intent,
on something in his own mind.
"I could walk along the Ridgeway," I said.

His head tilted and he looked along his nose –
a long nose, aquiline, a nose of suspension.
"No, you need to fly. Go to the pyramids.
Or, Pompeii. I often go there;
hop on the wing of an Alitalia jet
and slip off,
and glide down to the empty, night-lit Forum.
I like the place."

"Like me," he reflected,
flicking his ash on the carpet,
"you can think how well-preserved,
due to that incident, that event, and, like me,
you can people it with its old life again,
in your mind, in your mind's eye ..."
"I'm not sure," I said as he stood to leave.

And then
like a shooting star across the sky,
in a thought of 'what the hell',
I put my arm round Death
and we departed – each to
our separate path,
our individual way.

meeting himself

He thought he had recognised him, walking ahead
across the flags and the gravel towards the arch.
Walking behind, he thought he would be
as unnoticed as the silent crow.
But when the doors had slammed in this other's
face, and when the unfamiliar neck-line turned,
it wasn't meeting someone you knew or had once
known; it was the silent-eyed recognition
between strangers.

Each felt urged to grin and then to scowl
and then to lightly smile
but they gazed stone-faced;
they moved to leave the cool affection of the arch
and lightly touched through the knuckles of their
hands
and widened the angle of their leaving,
to be swallowed down different passages.
Perhaps,
if they met again, they might embrace.

in extremis

and always diving deeper,
there came a morning
when the light splintered on the
diamond shapes of the day
and knowing it was beautiful
but using ever deeper – in an
instant,
I gazed on a bed of gravel

shocked to find this limit
where no pearls are hidden, no
green slime smoothes each stone;
having ever fought to stay head
down, feet kicking above,
I looked around and there above me
crescent water shapes of light
ribbon eels of sun

quietly and deep inside
I put the world on hold,
and felt the body of the spirit
kick out to right itself
and then hang limp
to rise

I seek

to bring you pearls
from my diving.
I wrap them each in white tissue
and carry them in to you
and unwrap them before you
and wait for your reply,

and some, when I reveal them,
have left only a puddle in the paper
and I cannot make them hard
and whole again, but ask
for you to look at the water
and see the pearl

love and truth

love is not a contract
love is not a ring

love is not a set of conditions
not 'if'

love is not a transaction,
is not concerned with selling yourself long or
short;
love is not adoration;
love is or is not

love is receiving,
love is giving a stand –
it is a kind of truth
but more elemental, more precious

love is not peace,
love is not the holy ghost,
love is or is not

truth is a cloudscape, seeping into nothing,
blowing out of nothing, flowing,
swerving, diving;
like for the uncomprehending cat,
truth is, and is not.

True, love fades and burns brighter,
but when love hurts, it

does not hurt back;
love is not secretive,
love is not disloyal

You can find truth
- love, you learn.

luna et ego

By looking at the moon you know your self;
if its face is angry, you are angry;
if wide-mouthed with horror, fearful,
or it predicts the unrecognised
that may come to you;
if gaping and with mad eyes, you are lunatic;
if smiling, or with round cheeks,
the world is well and good may come.
It guides you in the day, unseen,
its cloudlike disk of presence in the blue. It
is the god that
moves and ripples in the waters of the
night lake, beneath the trembling surface
and above the deep.

elegy

Water was what I had been seeking,
warm-hearted lord of Nature,
naked to its centre.
But there were 5 miles of sand
between me and it,
or the water's edge was trodden and
aweless, a barrier.

Till the morning revealed the
timid moon murmurs of the night
as wind- and sun-enraptured hills and a light-
skating lake that
allowed approach.
The wind made no shadow on its water
that sailed with
light, and that, close to, drew back its reflection,
lying on its back and
showing to the spaces below, to the
shale, grey and still beneath.

Veering high in the hills there is another lake,
sepulchral,
fig-shaped and ovalled by trees;
it seems browned and muddy
when seen at first.
Yet, when seen on returning,
it yachts into view, its silken waters
intimations of reception and bliss
like fingers.

the weaver of myths

My body beside the gunnel,
I rest my head on the sea-leathered wood,
and watch the rending of the waters
and the dimples in the swell beyond,
and the ellipses of the waves as we hear the shore.
I lie back and view the motion of the sun's haze.

In the darkening I feel the ending of the voyage,
as we ride,
as the pilot weaves the shallows.

And in the night, I land
and sway on the still earth,
then sit to hear the creak and creak of the parting
oars.

Out from the rock shadows,
murmuring people come.
They sniff me and push me to their fire's light
where they know me
from my long nose and my high temples
as a spinner of stories;
they give me food. They ask me for my dreams.

I look at them as I eat and look at the moon
and know where the sun is.
The fire sinks low –
I raise my feet to it
and warm the crease below each toe,

and tell them of the woman
who crossed the desert alone,

and of how she came to a pool beside a strangled
tree, how the tree felt love for her
and watched her as she knelt and lowered
her mouth to the water to drink,
her lips raw.

My listeners murmur –
I tell them that as the tree gazed, a snake slid
from its roots
and climbed round and round her leg and entered
her.
And she ran to the tree
the tail thrashing between her legs, its head
engulfed.
And she grasped the tree and pressed against it,
and it moved
with her, and became man.

They look at me and question
"Is this true?"

"I am the weaver of myths," I reply.

sleep

to ricochet off waterfalls of light
cascading at the edge and end
of night, and glance off magma seas
of suns at ember; to be glimpsed
near glassy shores by eyes on stalks,
and by pterosaurs perched on pyramids of ice,
and,
to see them too, and feel the sirens' dark pull
lurk,
and know things slow to echo
of the coming crack

for me there is a star that draws me,
night-gliding, in,
then returns me from my dream-specked flight,
or gives another back –
wanderer of the milky way –
to link to vacant memory
of a distant yesterday

skim

Skimming's good – don't
look down – just skim.
There're grizzly things down there –
eel-y things, slippery things
with eyes all a-bate.
But, sometimes, there's
no wave to latch onto,
nothing convincing in its weight,
and you can feel toes
clenching in
down there in the deep,
as you wonder if that brush
was just the water,
or some seaweed tendril,
or some malignance,
or some fate ...

Part 3

In and out of time

eye

You on the up escalator, me
on the down – have we met?
do I know you?

did you
sell me something once? did we, in some
previous
reinvention, meet? Or,

was that glance, that
scythe, an abstraction, just
forgotten as soon as happen?

what is this?; an incising?; some laceration
in my heart?
Are you the moon veiled,

are you the sea? with the shadow on the sea-floor
of each craft, fishing in the night,
so that it floats, as if suspended,

air-suspended, beside the *Cinque Terre*,
the five lands, near Shelley's drowning, near
his burning on the beach,

where his body opened and
showed his heart,
the sudden silence of his heart

motion and sound

Flowers are inveterate chatterers –
you can tell from the way they bob about
comparing their profusion
talking of former lives
in hedgerows, and the turn of the year,
but what they love best is
to comment on the passers-by
and laugh at my enormity

But a single flower lodged in an asphalt
crack
will barely move
and holds a single note
as solace in its
solitude.

looking back

We'd kissed, bare-met,
in the station at Madrid;
we hoped we'd meet again
a day, a life, or two, later.
I waited for her on the platform at Granada
as the people came and never her.
I'd slept by another,
after meeting, in passing, on a train –
a brief communion,
as if always married,
as if hardly knowing,
and we danced with the Communists
at their gentle 'festa';
she wrote and I never found the words;
with another, I cruised
the windswept autobahn,
warm,
at peace –
in that little, yellow Beetle
that she loved so much –
through that proud and icy land,
and, upon the curve of her waist
I placed my hand ...
and when she said, what now?,
slight arch above her eye,
I could not find the words ...

I see them now, so far,
so far away like cream curtains flowing

in the wind, as I see this girl,
this woman on the cusp,
her face bare-lightly smiling,
her skin so pale and cloud-like,
her eyes and lashes
a flash of black,
her hair ashen –
in statement of herself so bright,
so elemental, so staccato-ed with dark,
so here

Beatore
(bay-ah-tor-ray)

I will always remember her,

Annalisa, standing in the street.
I would sit there in the evenings,
imagining the drab North London
suburb as a part of Italy,
while smoking, and drinking
a glass of wine. I enjoy
the company of waiters and
waitresses, but the best chats
were always with Annalisa – her long,
dark hair, the clench above her nose,
as she mustered all her English,
as she tried to make me see.

Once, late at night – when
I saw Ryman's across the road
as part of the Ligurian sea, and the
posturing kid-shopkeeper
threatening a Pole as Cosa Nostra,
and the pock-marked Indian lady in the 7/11
as a Neapolitan vendor in her
Tabacchaio – the talk between me and
Anna, me and Lisa, lulled, and I
just said, unprompted, to fill
the silence, 'Beatrice'. bay-ah-tree-chay

She lowered her gaze and smiled, "Beatrice

but also Beata - Beatrice is the giver
of blessings, Beata the blessed."
"And is there a male equivalent?" I asked.

Once more, between her eyebrows,
the little furrow. "Can Beata
and Beatrice be maschile?" mas-kee-lay
"You can be Beato, but no, there's
no Beatore." bay-ah-tor-ray
"Pity," I said, as she walked away,
her hips in sway, carrying her tray
to one side.

projection 2

in a green light, a tree spray,
an ivy amber, a distant
scatter of water, a playfulness
among white rocks,
dappled and flecked,
whiskers twitching
*

a thin sheet, still
and still moving, crystal
and glass, shatter and flash,
and beyond it and above,
rock, as continuous
and fleeting
as the spray below
*

the scalpelled
roots clutch the earth and, on high, the sky where
the branches flex and
sail the wind –
take this route
*

but the space is narrow – move
across the rutted tracks
to hedgerow, and stand
and stare at globe and petal, and see
close into the flower and shrink and settle
on the sepal of one,
so close that its yellow
is all around – consumes –

the yellow a bed of fur, the stamen
a pylon –
move legs and feel them six
and chew mandibles
and, beyond, see
mites – juicy, black grapes,
ripe beneath the leaves of a
mourning tree –
*
fall from the yellow
to the glow below and hit on
hard casing, legs
flailing, and think to hang
from inside the blue
of a hairbell, and see
a drone standing on the petals
of a poppy, as they tremble
like a ship in a storm-swell,
or a fly
perched on the purple red
of a tube of vetch,
upraised wings flexing – and,
a black shadow of bird,
mad bird, come over
and beak and let fall
into wrinkled, in-turned leaves –
take comfort in the red shell-casing
and the two black spots, sure
signs of foulness, and sense
the calling Skylark and the Swift
hold their distance

*

and, remembering, draw back
the wing cases and, hearing hinge and sinew,
draw out spider-web arcs
into the crystal of light,
and muscle-motion
into the sky

Miss

Some flowers there. White.
Indian white. White
from a hedgerow, tight twined,
snapped out.
I thought "Yes, better wild" as
I 'saw' her – sat beside the fire
in her box room; the glow
around the hearth;
a glance across the room – just eighteen.
Strange – she'd've been
almost sixty now.

Almost peremptory,
the way he said it, at the morning's assembly,
"Miss" – (Miss, miss, miss what, miss who?) –
"Miss
was involved in a car accident
last night. She did not survive.
She will not be coming back."
Three minutes. Three minutes' silence.
Was there?
"It happened at the end of Meadow Lane.
The far end. The distant end.
At the T-junction."
Strange. Strange, how you can say to the inner
soul: "No, no, don't go there."
Maybe, easier at nine.
It all came back to me –
a year or two ago, as looping

tendril, as light chance
through dim aquaria.

She wasn't double-barrelled, you see,
like that haughty pair who were there
before she came,
so gentle, so fine,
for that little time
– that brief time

honey on rocks

I bent down, in that café,
chasing the coin devils with my hands – like that
moment in Schindler's List, when he drops the
ring made from a filling – I bent down
and saw thin lines of light
through trees, as always when
I sense enrapture.

"Three pounds thirty," you'd said,
standing at the till,
voicing the 'th's, like in 'thine';
they weren't thin like in … well … 'thin'.
Maybe you knew they weren't right, and you
wished
it'd been 'two pounds twenty' or 'four pounds
forty', but
they were right to me.

The coins in my hands
had danced and floated into the air,
tricked me,
and now rolled like consonants
across the floor.
I was ashamed.

"You're losing your money,"
you chuckled – a waterfall
of soft laughter
down the shapes

of your words,
and the gravel shale
at the end of my soul
was splashed and filled over;
I looked down inside
and saw
liquid light.

I'd never heard you laugh before,
and now I wondered,
wondered at the honey,
the honey you knew
within you.

taking her to uni

"Hug"
That's what she said, when we'd moved all her
things from the car,
and piled them up in her room, in her single little
room.
You know, it had that intonation,
starting high and going low and rising high,
all in that word –
Hug

"Hug,"
she said, and I opened my arms and she
opened her arms, and one arm higher and one arm
lower in perfect match.
And,
we fitted together like cogs in a
gear, like
the upside-down 'u' to the block in a lock, and I
kissed her hair,
silken like an evening sea,
and when we released it was as if the chain was
released

"Hug," she said, with that intonation,
starting high and going low
and rising high, all in the word;
try it and echo it, like me ...

bird ascending

When I first …
called you, always a distant friend,
on your mobile
from mine,
to ask a favour,
having not spoken for years,
and you said

this and that and then
"oh my god", and
your voice was
like a cathedral window –
a red, blue, and yellow, and silver
glass of chords and light

I hear it now and
remember how I came to it, almost
came to it

And when your voice was
low, warm and cautious,
I felt you, something
in you, glow,
secretly on show

When I called to you,
it was like a bird
a skylark fluttered
from the darkness, and

it was a dark lark ascending,
and it was a dream
a dream that
could fall to the ground
in the morning

apart from 8

thighs tight, ankles like cricket's legs, shoes as
thin as needles,
hair blonde, cornfield blonde at late summer
sunset,
and roots night black
– sat at a table to my right -
resting her elbow on the velvet cushioned red,
as she told a story to her mates,
one on his mobile, of this guy in
New York who met this
hot bird – like, well, I mean hot – and got
syphilis – yeah, really – and she
laughed, her face youthful and perfect. Later,
one of the guys murmured something
and she fell lush
on the velvet and she laughed a stony, harsh,
endless
rattle of unmirth. Shortly they left –
she riding her bum out of there. I
sipped my tea and read some more of Love
Aware,
apparently so much better than the unconscious
sort,
whatever that is,
by two, who of course, like so much of
born-again Utopia, had found the light
and needed to 'best-seller' it to you. And I
read of all the 'snares' – from 1 to 9 –
as I worked through the cheesecake,

fork-slice by fork-slice, glistening
like a vanilla and cranberry Cheshire cat.
Trap-full, trap-shut,
I closed the book, and before me
were still a couple, their passing beauty further
tinged
by an endlessly-tried debate
and merely drooped now in a look of subtle
scorn.
At my gaze she glanced, with something
somewhere between
'fuck you' and 'I wonder',
or maybe she was just thinking of the … of the
'and'-ful days between them.
And between them, in another parallel plane,
a boy
who intoned and muttered by stages,
unnoticed, unrecognised, irrelevant –
like his yellow coat on the floor.
I opened the book again
and flicked thru' the traps.
Yep, I reckoned, I'm ensnared in all of them,
'xcept perhaps for no. 8.

if only

… somewhere – a soft-skin forearm, perhaps, –
on which to rest my head.
But then,
even if
head-resting there,
and though the air might be pensive
for a while – giving – then it would
restless and crease, and
there'd be something
chiding. Angels don't, I guess, lie on the ground
and let themselves
be a pillow,
a pillow for your head.

But I – yes, I can be an angel – I can
wrap my wings around you – feathers
splayed -
I can hold you, talons
tight,
tight around your waist,
and fly you up –
through the clouds
and the pearl glow
and lay you on a cloud bed,
where you could recline
supine,
and I, we
would steer with sail wings to the ocean,
and there, mid-sky, we would

hang over the curved and seeping
edge and see the dolphins
racing,
bottle nose to opal tail,
beneath the stillness of the sliding sea.

I am not there. I am
here –
here in the café, in the song, in the street, in the
screen,
in
the moment, in the white noise and
the rustle. And with muscle-hawsers,

my head sways, sways on its rocker,
all nerve-dream, all silent speech ... when dreams
take reign,
an end is near, I know

Christopher

I think the wailing started when I forced
you to a cold goodbye,
you to your bedsit, me to a glimmer and chime of
something. That
was the last time I saw you - me all unbrotherly -
a month or two before
you killed the noises in your head.
They say its doing is the shrillest act of
anger, the essence of revenge.
Are you avenged? Is it peace now?
No, I think the wailing started
when we passed on the basement stair
at so-called prep school, you hounded
by a bastard master on the way up
to punishment, me on the way down, intent,
passive-frightened, intent on some chord of a
chance ...
How did it feel? How did it feel to lay
your head on the line?
Could you feel the snap, the whip-snap on the
track,
as the train came towards you between the
suburbs,
the blank suburbs? Could you nurse and sing
yourself
in those hour-seconds?
No, I think the wailing started when we
came back from the heavenly Pradesh

to the UK, to school, and I wept and asked for
your kindness,
and you laughed, a monkey laugh, laugh of fear
and self-protection; or maybe
it was later, much later, like when we wrestled,
almost as adults, trying to make SOMETHING of
our pain.
      After you were safely boxed and
slid through the curtain, the wailing became a
feedback
of the heart, a rasping in the gut,
and it spread out from crevice to tunnel
to a swell and tide of howl-roar, that had
nowhere
to go.
      If I'm quiet now, so quiet as a
rat, always a rat, I still hear the wail, echoing
along the spirit's sunken ways,
like the squeal of the *Scalextric*,
our one point of silent harmony.

violentia

Smattercrash, the glass left your hand,
projectile at the cooker – and turning round your
twisted
grin, that 'see', that resignation of the slim
corners
of the mouth, that married look, that
speckled light

And again, I didn't see it coming, as just talking,
a kind of talking,
with wrists resting over the rim of the stillness of
the steering wheel,
while trying to float on smooth
psycho-sea, the knuckles in the face, left-hand
smash; it's
not the nerve pain at glasses driven
into nose bridge, bone ridge, that will stay, it's
the shattering of space, presence, sane assumption

That other time, the blows landed like mortar
shocks
on back of cranium, head-back, as my asking
"why?"… "why?"
"why do it?" in dull repetition & irregularity
matching the strikes,
and the smile that walked itself away and
turned with gleam prospect of one more strike-
chill
in the ringing dome, it abstaining,

as the innocent watch, bare-faced,
as ashen-foot tombs

That time, each time
stringing back, had been driven down, hammered
down, from
currency and mind
---
when
I open the door to me and look in, I see, I see
myself in self-reflection back in shards,
dancer crowded in with splints

You make sense of a button as you refrain,
retrain, as head down, acquiescent
to your noose of pain-strain, feeling
on another, another sea. No scope for beauty ...
now, not now, just staccato
and inner garbling, silent beat of drum,
and waiting till the gentle man visits in your sleep
and you have the dream,
the dream to leave, the dream
to be gone.

coming and going

Hang on a minute, this cannot be!
A second ago, there was nothing
except echoes of screaming, –
then silence and the wait for the bawling
that came thunderclap in instant to our worry,
and now there is you,
the unutterable suddenness of you, stilled,
your eyes like ice on a lake,
like soup –
what do you see, unblinking?

This cannot be!
A month ago, you were
all smiles and anger,
the wild distractions of you
filling my head and my spine,
and then you did start to lose it,
you'd come and go,
but I thought you'd come back,
not prepare
preparing us with what, what was to come …
And then of course, the news, and the going to
see. Ancient, unpretty,
locked in a stare, mouth silent-screaming,
eyes like ice on a lake,
like froth in the sea …
when we said goodbye and closed the door,
a kind of a whimper
– that was the door, I said.

early morning conversation - February

what are you doing there, sitting
in that chair? why are you all
dressed in black?
I have to go, go
to a funeral, to a funeral in a moment.
Inner moment.

did you know the person well?
oh yes, quite well, recently, and
some time ago

did you get on?
oh yes, I like to think so. we
had some great debates, she told
me things – explained things

did you argue?
I can't deny – we had a few
disputes. But, once, I said "I won't
argue with you now – in the end you're always
right, always right".

did you mind that?
not at all. she was my rock.
my redeemer.

an' what two things
do you remember most?
I think the way she treated everyone the same –

it didn't matter how 'big' or 'low'; to her you were
one the same. Each was each as one to one.
I think the way she did not measure out her love -
the show of love was neither here nor there, only
the
depth, and the tightness of its focus.

she has many friends, I'd guess.
Oh yes. But who are you, standing
here at dawn with me?

I'm the one that comes after - after the reaper. I
check the stubble,
I see the sheaves of feeling are in place,
I am the swell that brings no fear,
I am the tear.

at Munich airport ~ January

Beneath the cool serenity
of a still-distant sky,
below the tubing
and the crystal panes of glass,
Beside the anonymity
of the scanning arch,
the middle-eastern lady,
surprising, both guard
and handmaiden
– lush, brown, rich –
chocolate, date, and coffee - smiles,
with a slight ironic tint.
Life in a dead world.

"Remove your jackets, both,
and put your keys and coins
above them in the box."

… ebony hair and ice-pale
skin in piecemeal perception
behind me,
soul-close behind me … a distant
immanence, a tress of mind
… a small grey mole on her right cheek,
quite high, a dusky island
in a silver sea … a mourning squeal,
a cautious glance
from the quicksilver sun – and so,
I must be further checked

When spirits queue –
like Joan's Patrick, like Helen must,
just three weeks before, one night apart –
to board Charon's white new catamaran,
are they scanned
for some last morsel of life,
stealthed in a corner,
in the creased glint of a frozen eye?
Must they give it up,
every last twist, last sinuous strain,
before they embark,
heads searching through the window,
before they embolden
on the Styxian sea?

vergogna
(vair-gone-ya)

There are 7 paths around guilt - gilt-
edged guilt; the deep embedded sort that twilights
you
each morning after the day's brief crystal waking.
We can walk our way around - through meadows
of innocence.
We can deny. We can obviate
by doing good. We can deconstruct or

rewrite the narrative.

Or, we can use it as lukewarm purgatory,
and turn the hot tap
and the cold with our mental toe, as we
drift the hours by - future as entropy.

We can render guilty to deny our guilt.

There are no paths
around guilt. If there were, guilt would have
no function. It is its own end.
To live without peace and ...
can seem the only way: a stone in our shoe, a
bone spur, a
cramping of muscle and mind.

But, guilt is shared – guilt is a secret

compact.
We can weave shadows around us. We can offer
as truth what is lie. We offer it as stony-faced,
pure, transient, a cool, warm, diamond sea.

We can scour for clues, feel
the inner silence. ~ We
think to find others are true;
someone somewhere is genuine. ~
We seek to receive what we rarely
give from ourselves.
But, to be guilty is not the most evil, but to
have been. To be unguilty is.

~

Guilty guilt is handed on & down,
is passed between compatriots, siblings,
generations. It's 'pass the parcel'
and 'musical chairs', until choirs fall
silent, until the sad man, in *isola*,
says, yes, I accept this guilt, and will not pass it
on.

Have you heard?

Have you heard the whisper,
the whisper of the wind?
Have you heard it?
It comes behind you, and
once or twice, you sense it,
just behind your neck, just behind
your ear, a gentle prickling, just a
surreptitiousness, a kind of a
very, very quiet motion of the air,
like someone's there.
And look around,
and there is no one.

Have you heard the whisper of the wind?
Have you heard it? It comes just
once, just once or twice; it comes
when you have done that thing
that thing
you know you should have done
long ago,
long, long ago – have
you heard?
Have you heard it?

on the authority of children

the wine glinted,
just poured,
waiting like a mouth to be kissed ...
the mobile played Gould

hi, I was just starting to trust ...
how could you say what you said in your
voicemail?
I told you I didn't want to sort out your issues
with them ...

the sky of evening glinted ...

i can't remember what I said ...
i can't defend or fault what I can't remember.
i thought I was just giving information, not asking
for anything ...
maybe you should listen to it again.
okay so what's the new point?
so can I be blamed for breaking a rule I didn't
know existed?

all my limbs thrummed and shook like I was in
rocket climb - the stars seeped at the edge of
twilight

don't you see that could upset?
you're so immature ...do you think it's right to
laugh now? ... why be defensive?

the stars seeped at the edge of twilight,
like a self torn in two

And of course, a day later, the text ... *I over-
reacted, I'm sorry; I'll phone you tomorrow
if that's okay*

... and the stars came and went and the sun shone
like love, and slipped away again, and no call,
and the glass looked empty

not a poem so much as a letter

Well done, my sweet
– so well done.
I'm proud of you, not just for what you have
achieved but for what you are. It's amazing.
I can't see this keyboard
or screen through all these tears.
I won't go on – I don't want to embarrass you –
but for me you'll always be a star –
you always have been – not just for what you've
done but for what you are.
I'll always be in your debt
because you have the heart and grace
to give your broken dad
another chance.

You're free now to hurt,
to be, to cry with joy,
to find your pot of gold,
to chase your rainbow,
to explore all the spectra that are in you,
and find that resonance
with someone who speaks to you,
deep inside.

Stonehenge

Saw it yesterday,
saw it dip over the horizon – the horizon,
drawn down
like a falling curtain, like an easing open
of each eye.
It smiled, all hide, in the seizing
round of the sun – not so much
each stone in earth's pull but
in kiss-meeting, each meeting
in a moulding to the other,
new-touched, ever new-touching,
like moulded, settled clay – encircled
in itself, to count the movement of the
lights of every coming day
and night, a sighting and a mix
of sun and moon, of the mind's workings
and the spirit's sublime.

Simple in its way, its
circling, circled way –
an avenue of light where
the birds gather, black and silhouette against
the sky, that drops below our feet, withdrawn,
remote, awed, at bay – it makes
us higher than the stars at night
and moves the sun and earth
to shift and shift
their moment and their course, and
render it less seer of their

way, and more of deeper thought
than cool fore-thought of every silence
in eclipse
and of each midsummer's day.

the song of songs - V. 2.3

… what a beautiful and sacred place it was! Or,
so it seemed by what I and she would imbue it
with.
I walked around it nervously, and then I saw you
slip a glance across the nave at me …
Nonchalantly (almost unplanned), I sat to one
side,
one row behind, to where I knew you would be.
When you came back to your seat, I looked away
but then I watched you;
I tried to get the measure of you.
I always seem to get libidinous in churches; it
must be all that ecstasis in the air …

I saw you smile sweetly, reassuringly,
at your friend, as she prepared to speak her
chosen words.
I saw your bright, sharp eyes, as you turned to
her,
and felt the light and texture of your mind;
I saw the gentle, dark awe and curve of your
eyebrow
and saw your spirit;
I saw you stifle a giggle
at some oddity of word or event, and felt your wit
—
I explored you with my eyes,
your shoulders and upper back, the dark crease
between your arm and body,

the straps of your dress, the shapes and hues
of your skin like the dunes of the Sahara – you
had the aura of the Alhambra –
and your tattoo – the first tattoo I've ever loved.
Was this voyeurism, ogling?

It feels now more like veneration or adoration,
purest, gentlest love,
like preparing before the giving of confirmation,
and all beneath the stained-glass windows, red
and gold
in the light of the setting sun,
in that august, time-honoured space.
Finally, we spoke when the 'service' of jubilant
readings were over,
and, joy of joys, yes, you were coming to the pub.

And there, it seemed to take so little time
till we were deep in feeling,
and I can see you face-to-face, and start to sense
you
heart-to-heart,
and guess the contours and the flavours of you
from the movement and perfect shapes of your
mouth,
from the warm, moist taste of your breath in the
air.
And, there, it seemed to take so little time
before we were in deep discussion of you, and we
confirmed,
beyond all shades of a doubt,

that all was gorgeous.

I'd loved it when you felt I'd implied for you a
lack of full budding,
and as I tried to set the matter straight, you
murmured
"Dig that hole", and it felt like a
massive rush of love of feeling.
Your moonlight thighs – did shiver in the
summer's cool, as I saw
from the corner of my eye.
And we went inside so that you could be warm.

As we talked of this and that, and waited,
and as I enjoyed the pearl-glow of your teeth
and the shine of your mind,
I sensed you as a Contessa –
the 'bella figura', the 'alta cultura',
an Athenian queen, the Sicilian goddess,
my Cinderella, my first, my last, my only
Cinderella –
Were you half-flirting with that guy?
I kind of intervened, interposited.
He drifted away,
and you narrowed your dark, sly eyes,
as if to say, 'you can be a bit pushy' or
'I like it – am I getting your measure?'
And you smiled like the moon on the sea.

It was chucking-out time, and we went to see the
sea.

And we discussed whether I should hit someone
in the face,
for bumping, so jealously, into me.
As we passed some Italian deli
within the vivid display of shopping and
clubbing,
as you gently slipped your hand in round my arm,
so giving, and I pressed it lightly into me,
"Let's skinny-dip!" you yelled;
I did not know your name, then,
but waited till you would give it to me,
and then, so much later, I played with
how to rhyme to it.

Revelation,
like silent movement toward osculation
or solemn, joyful procession to any form
of con-gregation, all conjugation
should never be rushed,
for,
as with all the most sacred mysteries,
there needs to be time for the heart to become
as pure as it was, before, impure, through
wanting, wishing,
and for the trust to be as strong
as it was, before, unsure.

one and one makes four

High in the hills, there is a lake, a tarn;
I go to it to enter an ending, or a beginning,
like now.
Last time, there was sadness there,
and I left my she there,
the inner she in me.
But, without her, I was brittle and hard,
still aware not to be harsh or crude,
but not feeling so;
I was strategy and cunning.
I need her she in me to be in me,
to prompt me and guide me
to kiss your hand;
to caress away the tear from your cheek,
I need that.

I came again, now,
to reclaim her, so that
I can accept my gift, take my prize,
with a cry of joy, with sweet tears in my eyes,
and with lowered head, and on bended knee,
I give to you my me,
and hold your me in I.

inner chalice

is it like a libation?
does it grow red like wine?
and sometimes golden?
is it an urn in silver?

Alone – can one pour into it? What do you pour
from?
Can you pour from it?
Lift from it and soak it in?

It is a libation;
it grows red like wine;
and sometimes golden,
it is an urn of silver.

Alone – I cannot pour into it
nor from it. I can only look
at it, enjoy its amber glow.
Only in meeting, can I pour
from it and into it,
can I savour, and enjoy.

soundings

i

Over the sea - near the shell of rusted girders,
that gaunt skeleton of pier, where once they came
in throngs of bright eyes –
over the sea, she came. The moon lay with its
tip on the horizon, laying out
a clear path across the waves,
all the way to the shore and me.
Over the sea she came, stepping down
from the circle into the barge,
sudden pulled by loop-hugging dolphins,
all the way to me,
stepping from the floating shell,
and holding out her hand to me.

ii

Moon-flecked, she swept her hair
from before her eye, and looked at me,
as I took her hand and held
it before my lips, sensing
of their urgency, at the way
they curved round mine,
round my upper finger,
my thumb poised to touch
but not quite,
and saw a smile pass
across her face like a squall
across an evening's sea

and moved my lips above each
knuckle, each intimacy.

iii

And she turned, to look out on
the moon and the rising waves,
rising to our thought and feeling,
and the barge of shell was gone,
the dolphins withdrawn to the deep,
to lie sleeping below the rising
breathing, the restlessness,
the raising of the deepening sea.
Not knowing what force was in me,
what couraged me so, with this
unknown divinity, this dark Venus,
I moved close to, behind her,
and arced my arms around her
and watched the emerald of the moonlight.

iv

I arced my arms around her, and
against my racing skin,
I felt the curve of her,
the line and sweep of her back,
and placed my hands and fingers,
not knowing what could so
enspirit me, around the
globe of where, one day, her
babes would be, swimming
contented in their own inner sea,
and wondered at how she did not

argue or pull away, and felt
myself sink down into the rushing
pebbles, ankle-deep anchor against the sea.

v
I could feel the anger of the sea,
rising and rising at me,
angry and jealous at my bliss,
the greatest joy I had ever known,
might ever feel and know. I saw the waves rise
like a wall in front of me,
the top, white-flecked, surf with eyes
like those of ghosts, of mischievous
spirits, foam-flecked black orbs,
eyeing me and her to see
what they could do to take her from
me, just met, just so deeply
known, and the cruellest monster
came and flicked her sideways like a feather.

vi
I jumped my hold, to hold her,
her waist, as the great wave of
crashed and hurtled over us,
and waited and waited for the dreaded
tow, the great pull of the undertow,
the pebbles crashing and hunting for
my heels, the Achilles in me –
I felt her trust to me,
and felt her surge at the jealous
love of the ocean's arms

straining to pull her from me,
so only met, so newly held, and so very soon,
it seemed, to be hurled from me
and dragged into the cavern of the sea.

vii
I held her tight; she got her footing
and sank back into me,
the water lurking quieter at our ankles –
and the next rising and the next seemed calmer,
gentler, till a sudden stillness
spread across the water from the horizon
to the edge, and we waded in, deeper,
and linked just hand-in-hand,
side-by-side, and then she
turned and, face-to-face,
we looked each other in the eye,
we linked both hands,
we brought our lips to touch,
to nestle in the touch of love.

he and she

he

I am the glint of the morning sun
that slants through the gap in the curtain;
I move in slow motion across your cheek
as you measure the dawning.

I am the clock that ticks you into your waking.
I am the mirror that holds you in frame.
I am the bee that nectars, I am
the warm cup you hold in your hands,
watching the sun's rising.
I am the warmth of mid-morning on your skin.
I am the one that holds you
with quiet palms and warm and gentle fingers.
I am the one that you hug, when I am
stooped and lingering.
I am the one that listens
as you cry out in the night,
as you murmur your dreams
to the sleeping clock.

I am the road you speed along.
I am the mind through your hair.
I am the sand on which you tread.
I am the tree that shades you
          when the heat is too strong.
I am the rays in the water of the sea,
when you dip your toes into me.

Into you – I glided,
unknown, beckoned, unapprised.
In you I found my me, and
gave to you my I
and, if love should light your eye,
I'd hold your I in me.
In you I stand, in you I rise,
and feel you
glow in me.

she
I am the coursing in your veins,
I am the blood through your heart,
circling round and round,
through every pore, through every mound.

Is this the end of our story, or the beginning?
It feels like a mystic moment,
like a birthing – I feel the
acts of nature, moving,
sacred, and precious – there is
a hush – concentration
and focus as a chalice of spirit is carried
through the air, to some form
of arriving, some sense of
moving, from doing to being.

I am the whisper in the wind,
I am the breeze on your arm,
I am the sense of someone,

someone kissing on your cheek,
as you lower your lids under the weight of my
breathing,
as you nestle
and flow to the way I hold you,
so peacefully.

dove

She talks to me, you know,
quietly, calmly, simply –
she loves you so.
She was so worried about you,
just a week or two ago.
She's calmer now.

She remembers when you hurt your knee
and you ran to her (a blur
of rushing legs, the sun all silver in your flying
hair), and
she put you on her knee
to comfort you ...
and then sat you opposite
and removed the grit,
and you winced,
and she put on the ointment
and a little plaster,
and you started talking again

and told her how much you loved her.
She talks to me, you know,
calmly, quietly, not stressed,
not now – it was just,
just that she loves you so.

She thanks you so,
for being brave and kind and honest,
gentle to the guy, the silent guy;

she says she's always there,
just behind or to one side –
she says you're not alone;
you're deeply loved,
loved by so many.

clush

There's a ring around you spreading out in tides
and ripples and sparklets of you –
I felt it from far, from the distance, the 'lontano';
you gave a subtle wave, as you turned the corner,
and strode, almost bounced, across the square;
but, I'd felt the ring like a tug of spring across
my skin and,
from its curve, knew you its centre before the
hand-raise
across the flags – the sign of you.
In close – now – then? – all now is then – a brush
of hand – did mine hold yours? –yours mine?
Was it? Is it?
A touch of hand – hand in hand – yours
in mine – mine in yours? But – unplanned –
unthought – unthinking –
dream-lost, dream-found in passing, in moment
of passing –
some momentum, some hand in the small of me,
powered
me to cheek to cheek – no aura, none of that –
just,
just cheek-sting, cheek- scratch, but I noticed it
then, here
at the sun's core, the clash of core to
Venus, of anima to soul; I felt your soul cry out
across the square, through the dawn of circles and
rummage around

the alleys, earthen and Saturn, the dark alleys in me.

the icy claw

The icy claw is not a fear of love,
so much as of love's agenda.

When only have we received it
within some feeling 'commerce',
when love has only been conditional,
then, of course, of course, it is icy,
a glacier of the system,

it grips the sinews of our heart so bright,
it makes the pain so tight,
we cannot think,
we cannot think.

We cannot breathe
with all that makes us want delight.

in spite of the difference in age

grateful:
for our years of secret communion –
how you were always thoughtful,
all insights and gentle reflection –
no grand philosophy, just moments
of introspection

And moments of sharing, of declining from
posture
and parade,
always sensing the need for humility,
always distrustful of display, always
questioning the seeming roots of acts and views,
always honest

I can't say this any better, no grand words or
moving imagery, just simple thoughts and simple
thanking, for what you gave and gave to me.
Each time I raged against this
love, it was because I could not
trust, I could not see the
care, and the seeking of your own
redemption, and can only speak now in silent
supplication … to a ghost that once was
here.

until I looked at you

"Oh yes, it's yours", they said, "we were about to
leave", giving us the bench – you smiled cutely
like a Jedi placing thought in others –
we sat and talked in that London square, high
gate to your soul, and the late
autumn evening sun crowded you –
I thought love was caverns –
I gave you my straw hat, and its shade
made a tracery across your eyes
as you took me to the 'naughty' niches
of your soul and told me of the
things you'd done – but I felt nothing
as I lost myself in the chestnut glow
in each basking pool of your eyes where angel
motes,
crystal white, seemed to fly and the skin sheen –
another time, your temper flared, another time
traces of anger and hurt smouldered, like a comet
across the sky, but I felt nothing –
I thought love was holes, with tight seams you
sidle through,
where you lose the air as you dive into black
water – till ...
– I felt this simple glow when, out
of the blue, you just texted "Hallooooo!", and,
foolishly, one day later,
when I texted back a gentle "Boo!" –
but there is something I still don't understand,
like a climber clinging on to old and anxious

ways, 'why me?' 'why, ON EARTH, me?' –
and I've lost the feather they gave me
to remind me of that time you picked a feather,
"that's a good one" saying, from the ground
and placed it in the flowing, in-flowing, curving,
in-curving
of the soft braiding of the dark lush
of your hair

Was it?

Was it some god that threw that faint spray
of light, bright freckles across your chest, that
night sky where the stars are dark
and the dark is light?
Sun spray, sea spray, light spray, dark spray
where luscious and luscious ever
meet, I confess my
eyes wandered down when
you, looking down, drew triangles
to work out the shapes
of my path and numbered the characters
of my way, and, though I still wonder as to who,
then I knew that my
destiny was done and that I was just a kid
left to play, stay, stand and sway
long after my dark was planned to come and,
looking at the curve – sun spray, sea spray
light spray, dark spray
where luscious and luscious ever
meet – before your heart,
that my destiny was won.

the times of ages

In life's morning,
when the dawn has passed
and the world is becoming lit,
pure sense hits;
and in that brief
and feeling moment,
we lift our feet and
trust to the swell and kick out
to swim

Alone and exploring,
that time came to me, like it came to you,
in the late early morning heat,
alone and free,
that knowledge came,
that knowing
of who we are, and
who we are to be

And then,
when pregnant with middle age,
I feel my father
and his mantle
draped across my shoulders,
and seem to me
as he seemed to me,
self-pleased and satisfied, and yet

uncertain,
watching my children find their way,
sensing their belief, their
half-belief that I will always stay
mid-ocean, as
I did of my father,
feeling their feeling that
the waves of me are purposeful
and untravelling,
lifting up and lifting down
through the endless passage of
bare-changing days

Limp, facing down,
carried by black crows
over the rank vegetation where snakes look
skyward,
along the track of thorns
and splintered glass
out into the plain
to the tower of silence,
to be picked clean.
And, I will feel the waves of me
hammering into the shore
and there at the edge, above some cauldron inlet,
I will see my children unseeing in the mist, and
some of me will linger with them
as spray and tumult,
troubled with care,

gentle in that night,
and some of me rebound
to where the half-life roams
and the rock core sleeps.

.

chemistry

The snow came in the night to bless us.
Hope we are blessed, but it seems as if.
The dawn was a cream on the crumble of night.
Crystals formed in silence and reverie and
expectation of the forming day, the sound of
your text in my eyes
as grey shades watched me watch the coming of
day. I walked through the all of the ice-froze
weeds
along the raised path to the circle of steps.
Fox-print set silent in the iced step,
night movement frozen into the sight
of dawn like the secret working you entail in
my own garden's soul as I dream-breathe and feel
you, alone,
angel-step your spirit through me, a dark pool
breathing in the moonlight and heart of your steps
through your own distance and night.

Down from the terrace through the psychic stress
of wishing light, the deer print, silent witness
to their path across the frozen lines of
grass.
You have been here too – saw you,
in the glow of summer, in the thunder of that light
and skin,
in the hunt for fruit amongst these trees.
Will we walk again here, you and me, next
summer,

you ravishing the yew in me, the distant witness
to you,
where I walk now through the dark arced
passages,
knowing you near and far?

beauty

And, we had some good things didn't we? I loved the way
you leant into me that time, shoulder to
shoulder when I sat beside you in the glow of
morning.
– the way that she told me
that you fretted that I wouldn't find you
when you were sitting on the beach
and'd moved your sunning spot.

– the way you prepare in the morning for each
day, the way
you think about your clothes and how you then
rethink them. – the way you'd throw yourself at
me, spraying me
with cold water from your dark and showered
hair.
– the way you
smile when you're released and expecting. – the
way
you think in your face, all feelings in your face. –
your purpose when
we have planned an assignation. – when you're
cold with me,
as it makes the warmer more subtle, more
precious. – the way you make it, seeing your face
above me or below
deep inside
thereelings of your own filling and joying.

121

– the
surprise you imply in the tips of your lips and eye
when you are wavering and resolving. –
your
entrance that cups my hood before allowing
further. – the way she shows when she has
done enough. – the curve of your doves, the point
of them,
rawness and surface and how they grow and
respond like thoughts to a feeling. – your navel
like the cove at Tintagel. I love
your arms and shoulders, your thighs, all and
every bit
of you. I love your voice that entrances me
with its poise and humour. – the sharpness to
your eyebrows when you're holding something of
yourself,
and taking note of an inner thought. –
your high cheek bones, your lips and tips of
tongue. – your
sway in your hips as you walk ahead of me;
– the smile in each crease. –
the sculpture of your eyelids, the depth between
them and
brows. – your hair, its darkness and waves. – the
way you look at yourself
as you dry your hair and then the angle of your
body
when you touch up the skin near eyes. I love to
watch

you walk from the land into the sea, the
movement of your
hips, the angle of your back.
And yet, and yet, maybe,
the physical is enough, but not for me,
when I have, before all this, felt the glow,
implicit,
of gentleness and care with another random other.

fare...wells

... "It's a bit like trying to get
out of a swimming pool," he said,
his back against the wall, bricked edge
eating into his small-ness, palms
resting unused, elbows angling towards the sun.
"Yeah, ... and hoping no one will
notice," she said, draining away along
the raised walk, the yew shades dark and
pleading like her soul. And,
the constellation of night shone briefly
through the cloud, the murk of the
day, and the sprite light sparkled and
wept.

"Yes, ... a bit like trying
to get out of love," he said inside,
the clouds a held thought, easing
himself up and out, palms
flattening onto the crusty, crannied brick,
out from the semi-circular space, cedar
centred; it had turned around him
as he waded through the lush of nettles,
nestling around a small silver, cream
fleck of remembrance fastened to
the slightest stick, a note to note
where the ashes had poured, dust
to earth, ashes to stems, feeding
pin-snips into life.

"Who is it?" she would say, as
you eased the door open, to ask her
her wishes, and her trapped by age into staring at
the blue sky, at the screen of flash and image,
pin-pricks of intensity. "It's me."
And then, it was "I need you to find ..."
... to find the accoutrements,
the appurtenances, lost, displaced, disarrayed.
And then,
the time to marvel at her mind, at
the sparkle in her eyes, the constellation of night
shining through the murkiness of day. You
came to help but you came to be healed.
The pin-pricks and pin-snips, the barnacle
accretions,
the quiet that she brushed away.

Each ... each meeting is a life
and a death – the tunnel opens from the
darkness into the light, flecks of warmth across
the soul's skin – exposed and translucent - the
blood flows, the heart talks in a stutter and
stammer. And then, back into the
dark as the pupils widen
and the unsaid is unspoken.
They feel and know this moment, soul-etched
forever,
the she easing along
the walkway, and away, into new experiences,
expectant of new hushes and tremors in the dark,
and the one releasing up into the beckoning sky.

coda/headrush

Between the silence of lips along the slide where
a kid had slid along that black-lined
-strewn, -tickling, -prickling, -pricking,
star-lit avenue, I felt the inner piece of you, your
closed true-ing, being, flower that sucks the
honey like seed, your
mind foggy, hazy, bare-lit like a Berlin fifties
street; I felt your deep stream, your pale
electric ultra-violet of proto-mind, of bare-lit self,
in that private and slick of silk – that cream-mind
– though
I know you know, in your cream-midst,
the plays of thought-vice – while your song, your
sung, is flung through equal bars that we, your
seekers, have made and make for you. Still,
yours is the spreading constellation star-struck,
-stricken, that perfect peace, that fortune, that
liquid piece of rhythm expressing, holding tight
– through circles of being, teaching, history, that
infection of past, retraining – and stays a pale,
deep subtle of
violet light. Yes, I am Egypt to your Roman,
germain and silent, like your Turk, taken in the
silence of lost, half-forgotten night, I am
Jew to your easy Venetian, a Montagu
to your Capulet, I, a Capulet to your Montagu,
your arms once uplifted as you let me slide things
away and up you, a sonnet, all 14 lines round
this, my in-peering eye, your Stazi, your

mechanic, tight-squeezing your sleepy buds,
raising into rising, surprise and wince in
your eye and breath; blotch and arse-face
mechanical, I am the you you never hoped to
meet ... that big uneasy question ... I am how
difference meets and melds, and they meet in me
when they meet in you ... even in that silent,
lonely flat that sits and broods like a cell of cells
in a Gulag, where the grass sits perfect, waiting
for wind and breeze that never comes, near that
wide and streaming river that flows silent as the
night in the deep of sunlit days, whose breasts sit
in folds ... I am big-head and humility, meek
and idle mild and pride, and price waiting
to be unpaid, yet and so, I am vengeance, dressed
as
love and other way around, and am I am when I
am in you. I am, now, and I thank you, even and
in spite, though I am not worthy to be your
germain, your due, your Capulet, your disdaining
Montagu, your passion due, your scales, your
mechanic, your mechanical, your God, your
power, your light, your shit-storm, your enclave,
your ghetto, your slave – even, as you release the
hawk and let him go into the moon-sipped void,
with precipice and god-head's reflection gone,
knowing only the unelected self ... peace, where
no caged birds sing ... but still,
in the grave of ticking night, in the silent
Cyclops' eye of mind, I put my jealous palm
along your lips, your line of flower, and you raise

your brooding thumb and fingers, from your side,
delicate and precise, and hold me there.

Lara

"You have done all this before", she said,
claiming she did not mind, denying any
needle of hurt in her heart.
Was I a fake, I mused
in the silence before reply, did I, each time,
take out love's hypodermic and
press it into old veins running cold, did I
only project onto each new, blank canvas
that came my way?

"All your muses have dark and wavy hair," she
said,
pulling at the straight, silk auburn of her own.
I had no answer – nothing to say –
a springing fox caught. A vacant 'criminal', I ran
through an excuse like moving fingers across a
brow:
"my anima has dark and wavy hair – raven
hair and exotic eyes; I looked for her, but I do not
now,
she is of the past and gone." Relaying messages
to and fro across nerve ends, I frantic chorus,
I wondered myself to be just loving
love in all those times and places, a psychic
Casanova, just for the tremble
in the veins,
the focus and shining in each moment's heat.

rich dad, poor dad

Rich dad had it all, the sheen
of the thick white walls inside the extensive
property with the perfect Jekyll garden,
the sheen of the newish car and Bauhaus oven
and hob and stereo and telly, the sheen of the
lush bank balance, the sheen of the
investment accounts, and the sheen
of the tanned skin of the ever-so-polite
financial advisor, ever-so-your friend and loved
one.

Yes, there was the perhaps-more troubled son
with his
strange events and sagas,
the sudden midnight
vomit on the stairs, the air-letter where
each
inch was filled with the meaningful words of
'bla bla bla',
the spitting on the dashboard - but, these were
passed, passed by, like an anonymous drunk in
the night.
And yet, other anonymi had been saved and, yes,
a flat was bought to house him, reducing his
presence to visits.

Rich dad filed all his inbox and assembled photos
in albums of family history and catalogued the
old cine films of visits and smiles and dramatic

little sagas. And then, the day came, the twilight,
when the son visited and complained of the
endless
noise in his head and they pleaded with him, rich
dad
and rich mum, not to disappear into the night,
but he went to his ending, to his own planning,
and then
the phone call and the voice, too loud, too soft,
too hesitant, too determined, harsh
in
its words of sudden reality.

In later years, rich dad would recatalogue and recollect and recollect the times and faces
in the picture manuals, the joyous story books
of growing and changing, that would show back
that face,
now no more ... He wept inside, allowed himself
that even,
while still showing perfect to the world.
Poor dad had little, and even meagre hope when
the inheritances from rich dad filled briefly his
account, that always plunged back into a
withering 'red'.

In a 'lusher' time, poor dad got the call; it was her
who had almost spurned him, while he had
worked to prepare
for the moment of crisis. "Dad, I need your help."

He muttered something, thinking this not yet the
nadir
but just a portent. "No, Daaaad, I really need your
help."
So this was it. He drove to her. He found her.
Together,
they grew. Together, they learnt to understand ...
each other, their woe. And slowly, two more of
his came to him.

And, with each, he said, at different times "I'm
sorry I've not been perfect,
I'm a struggling mortal, like you – more so."

And now, he found under the papers of the
debt-management plan – 4 years in, 3 still
to run – a tangled mass of atrophying plastic,
a swallow of photos.

He found an album, barely used by some other,
in a pile in a heap, and built his own collection
with the shine of young and perfect faces,
sequencing from year to year,

for each to see when they were ready.

heron?

So many, by now, have passed on, passed on
from me.
"Well," I murmur in myself, "shall I speed the
process on, me too?"
when, so many times,
the passing was brought on,
hurried on
like a shedding of skins, a relinquishing of coils,
a final bid
for clarity.

And, then, nature obstructs, saying
"I don't acknowledge you, but look at me!"
as with the bird that passed
overhead,
but something exotic,
its neat complex of claws
picked out against a greying darkness of sky,
intense in contrast and definition,
hanging from the arches of its wings,
balanced in precision at its beak;
a heron?, I yell inside, a reminder of life,
a poised magnificence

But why, why the silent intake, the wonder,
the elevation at this reveal,
this scope for silence and exultation?
Does the intensity of life lived,
gain traction from knowing they are dead,

locked out of sentience,
of beauty, of awe only felt
when played across the thrilled senses?

But, what says they cannot soar, cannot look
through my eyes and,
prompted, feel their own joy?

Wondering what happens in the next-after,
I seek to hold onto this that I have,
in this now,
in case it will be lost to me, if I am,
as with all others perhaps,
to become cerebral, mental, all mind,
within the unknown of what borders
this brief play in time.

unthankfulness

I said: Why did you pluck me out?
Why did you end my seeming eden, my atlantis –
as amethyst wrapped in cotton wool?

He said: Did you not want to live?
Were you not in a mesmerised eclipse of the
heart?
Were you not happy when you saw the exit (when
you felt the sage visiting the bull seeing it forlorn
and bespattered and said "look! - the gate is
open") and you took it?

I said: I guess so. But, I didn't expect it to be so
much of so many hours – intermittent,
interminable.
So many moments of shoring up some narrative
to myself – frail, weaving in the dark.
Joyousness perhaps – but also, all so joyless.
So much tense waiting, the hours trickling
through sleep – the seeking to live with knowing
the unknown.

He said: I didn't promise you an elfin garden. I
sought to give you life. I felt the yearning. I felt it
for you. I wrapped it in tissue and gave it to you.

Death sighed and gathered himself and left,
irritated perhaps at unthankfulness; though, like a

father, he didn't so show it. In me, there was a
slim sliver of guilt.

I said: Oh well, we will meet again on my final
day or my last night – that is
        a certainty, is it not …

vanity of disdain

Death provides no ready path;
he gave me that chance
to bathe in ecstasies, to
nestle in extremes,
the chance to show signs of weakness,
signs of woe, to breathe in
each squall, each salt mist,
each unchartered hope
to bathe in ecstasies, to
nestle in extremes, and feel him let me know
when the scope for hope is gone,
in each blantant moment of quietude and raging,
each resignation and indignation,
and to know the vanity of disdain,
on that journey I did not know,
I did not know I had to take.

(acknowledgment to Blake's 'London', for the echoes)

appreciation

Acceptance ... is a kind of charity, a charity to
others. It's like to say you do not need to
lie for me, you do not need to glide around
my locked heart. It's like to say I do not
need to waste away.

The spirit cannot accept – it cannot pass away,
all pinnacles and chimes, olives,
minarets, and azure seas.

But, it will listen, and only when the soul draws
in
a breath and says, hush, be still and shut your
mouth, focal point of tasting and expressing –
that constant overweening.

We can lean to others and learn;
but, when they say, away, be gone and
shut up your shop ... and we return to another
year alone,
that's when we need to choose our path, to seek
to soften and soften
out the days with chanter once again, or look in
and silent survey and think to think
no care or blame away,
to seek no ease but search the truth, pick through
all its pockets, shuffle around through
all those receipts and draw
in, tense and tension,

like a suspension of a bridge, and cantilever the
spirit to the soul and
accept.

When does hatred come?

Where does hatred come from,

and, then, the impulse to
revenge,
not just to bully, but to
avenge?

It's designed to settle the score,
when found wanting.

You can see it in the spouse's
prayer,
to effect annihilation on the other, the partner,
their
pair.
It's in the mother's
lament,
that leads to the passing on of
guilt,
where the offspring, the child, is made carrier
of the parent's
shame.
It's in the lover's pride,
who feels rejected when laid
aside,
and needs to know the hurt they deal
is more than that received.

But, each hurt can just be written in each vein,
sluggish but not dead;
each can be held, for no further transport on,
no victiming of yet another – in silent reception,
acknowledged and known,
recognised,
but not sent, sent on

Printed in Great Britain
by Amazon

22737572R00079